Mr. Yowder
the Peripatetic
Sign Painter

Holiday House Books
Written and Illustrated by Glen Rounds

OL' PAUL, THE MIGHTY LOGGER

LUMBERCAMP

PAY DIRT

THE BLIND COLT

STOLEN PONY

RODEO

WHITEY AND THE RUSTLERS

HUNTED HORSES

WHITEY AND THE BLIZZARD

BUFFALO HARVEST

LONE MUSKRAT

WHITEY TAKES A TRIP

WHITEY ROPES AND RIDES

WHITEY AND THE WILD HORSE

WHISTLEPUNK OF CAMP 15

WHITEY'S FIRST ROUNDUP

WILD ORPHAN

WHITEY AND THE COLT-KILLER

WHITEY'S NEW SADDLE

THE TREELESS PLAINS

THE PRAIRIE SCHOONERS

WILD HORSES OF THE RED DESERT

ONCE WE HAD A HORSE

THE COWBOY TRADE

THE DAY THE CIRCUS CAME TO LONE TREE

WILDLIFE AT YOUR DOORSTEP

MR. YOWDER AND THE LION ROAR CAPSULES

THE BEAVER: HOW HE WORKS

MR. YOWDER AND THE STEAMBOAT

MR. YOWDER AND THE GIANT BULL SNAKE

Mr. YOWDER
THE PERIPATETIC
SIGN PAINTER

THREE TALL TALES
BY
GLEN ROUNDS

HOLIDAY HOUSE
NEW YORK

To Mary Q. Steele with much love,
and fond memories of that hot afternoon so long ago
when I painted the Bull Durham sign
on her grandfather's store in Little Bug Tussel, Tennessee

Copyright © 1976, 1977, 1978, and 1980 by Glen Rounds
All rights reserved
Printed in the United States of America

Library of Congress Cataloging in Publication Data

Rounds, Glen, 1906–
Mr. Yowder, the peripatetic sign painter.

CONTENTS: Mr. Yowder and the lion roar capsules.—
Mr. Yowder and the steamboat.—Mr. Yowder and the giant
bull snake.
[1. Humorous stories. 2. Short stories] I. Title.
PZ7.R761Mn   1980   [Fic]   79-18387
ISBN 0-8234-0370-X

Contents

A Few Words
from the Author

It is a fact that sign painters nowadays are pretty dull fellows, as a general thing. Many even wear white shirts and neckties to work, have air-conditioned offices with telephones, and a lady with a typewriter to write letters and send out bills. Mostly you cannot tell them from ordinary people.

But at the time I speak of—which was a long time ago, before the country filled up with radios, television, automobiles, and computers—things were different.

The sign painters in that day, like the scouts, trappers, keelboatmen, loggers, and locomotive drivers of the better known tall tales, were a special breed of men. They had been everywhere and seen everything worth seeing. At least most of them claimed to have done so—which amounts to practically the same thing.

They traveled north and south and east and west across the country and, wherever they went, the people of the small towns welcomed them as eagerly as they did the dog and pony shows, the tent revivalist, or the chautauqua. There wasn't much in the way of entertainment in those places, and the coming of the sign painter was an event to be endlessly talked of and discussed for weeks after he had done his work and gone.

To watch such a man take a piece of chalk and casually sketch in the letters of a sign on the shining glass of a storefront was a magical thing, well worth seeing. There would be a respectful and breathless silence while he made his way carefully through the crowd of men and small boys to stand on the curb for a critical look at his handiwork. And when, after making a small change in the outline of a letter here or there, he opened his battered box and began searching among the small cans of paint, the crowd would press close to watch his every movement.

By the time he had selected a can, opened it, and stirred the paint until it met his approval, most of the storekeepers up and down the street had probably come out to join the watchers. Even the banker would more than likely find some excuse to come out and watch.

At last, the sign painter selected a brush, dipped it into

the paint, and drew it back and forth across a piece of cardboard until the bristles were flattened to exactly suit him. Then, when he was sure that every eye was on him, he faced the glass and in one firm, sure stroke drew a line from top to bottom of the first letter, flicking the brush out to the left at the last moment in a neat, sweeping curve.

It was truly a thing to see.

Stroke by stroke the outlines of the letters appeared, one after the other, as if by magic. The straight lines were straight and bold, the curves fat and round, and the points sharp and sure.

After all the letters had been outlined and filled in, there were borders, shadings, highlights, and decorations to be added—while the spellbound crowd watched every motion. It was a sight one didn't see every day and nobody wanted to miss a single detail.

But, best of all, while giving the people this glimpse into the magical world of art, the sign painter both entertained and informed them by sharing with them his vast knowledge of the world.

As he worked, and during the times he took for a little rest, or to select another brush, he spoke of unusual signs he'd painted in this place or that. He mentioned the names of far-off towns as casually as the local citizens spoke of neighboring farms. At mealtimes or during evenings on the boarding house porch, he was always the center of a crowd of respectful listeners fascinated by his tales.

He would describe great cities like Amarillo, San Antone', Kansas City, and a hundred others in such detail that his listeners could almost see the streets and houses. He knew where all the railroads ran, and could give eye-witness accounts of great floods, fires, train wrecks, and other catastrophes the listeners had only read about in the papers.

At one time there were hundreds of these fellows drifting about the country—all of them splendid craftsmen and master storytellers. But probably the best known of them all was my old friend, Mr. Xenon Zebulon Yowder. He spoke of himself as being the "World's Bestest and Fastest Sign Painter," and perhaps he was.

Our trails crossed now and again in Missouri, Kansas, Texas, or the Dakotas—and at various times we even traveled and worked together (I, too, was in that business for some years) for a few days or a week. So I heard at first hand the details of dozens of the fantastic things he'd done. A lesser man would have been accused of "drawing the long bow"—of stretching the truth, or even downright prevarication. But Mr. Yowder's very appearance inspired belief. And with the possible exception of a few harmless embellishments here and there, I think his tales were probably very, very close to the exact truth, in all respects.

In the years since I last saw him (in Peculiar, Missouri it was, or maybe Chugwater, Wyoming), I've read dozens of accounts of the fabulous doings of such characters as

Paul Bunyan, the inventor of logging, Mike Fink, so-called "King of the Keelboatmen," Davy Crockett, Jim Bridger, and other such adventurers.

But nowhere have I found any mention of this long-time friend, Mr. Xenon Zebulon Yowder—KING OF THE PERIPATETIC SIGN PAINTERS. Yet he, too, was a man who, in his spare time, did seemingly impossible things as regularly and easily as ordinary men tie their shoelaces in the mornings.

So, being as I'm probably the only person who still remembers him, I've written down here three of the more believable of his amazing (but true) adventures.

GLEN ROUNDS

Mr. Yowder
and the
Lion Roar Capsules

At the time I speak of Mr. Xenon Zebulon Yowder, the sign painter, was living just outside Lee's Summit (or Peculiar, or Gunn City or some such place) in Missouri.

This was in the time of what was later called The Great Depression—a time when almost nobody had any money to speak of—and a great many had even less than that. So, not having money to spend, people had gotten into the way of trading things they had but could get along without for things they needed more. This was known as Taking in Trade, or Barter.

Even in hard times such as those, people in business had to have a certain number of signs painted, and Mr. Yowder managed to stay right busy. Sometimes he was paid in cash for his work, but mostly he simply took whatever useful items a customer offered instead. What he couldn't use himself could eventually be traded off to someone else. But in the meantime finding a place to store these things came to be something of a problem.

When he'd first come to town Mr. Yowder had rented a nice room from the Widow Lucas. The Widow was an understanding woman, and she said nothing the day she was sweeping out his room and found he'd stacked six bushel baskets of apples and a bag of Bermuda onions in the corner beside his bureau. Nor did she say anything later when she found a crate of eggs, an old set of buggy harness and six cedar posts stored under his bed. She knew that in times like those a man had to take whatever he could get in return for his work, and so far Mr. Yowder had always managed to take in enough cash to pay his room rent each week.

But even so, she was a neat housekeeper, and there was a limit to her understanding. And that limit was reached the day she found six Rhode Island Red hens and a young tom turkey shut in his closet, and a big gray goose walking around the room hissing at her when she tried to sweep. That evening she told Mr. Yowder he had to move.

Mr. Yowder agreed that the room *was* getting just a mite cluttered, perhaps. And, furthermore, that very day he'd taken in four Pekin Ducks and a small goat in payment for a sign he'd painted over in Raytown.

So he loaded his things into the back of his old car, said good-bye to the Widow Lucas and moved out to an

abandoned farm just past the edge of town. Nobody was using it at the time and he had plenty of room to store his growing collection of things taken in trade.

As I say, in spite of the Great Depression Mr. Yowder was doing right well. Around the barber shops, filling stations and feedstores men told one another that there was nothing, no matter how unlikely, that Mr. Yowder wouldn't take in trade for painting a sign. And always, they said, he'd somehow manage to make at least a small profit on the deal.

Almost everybody agreed that, one way or another, Mr. Yowder would one day be a very rich man.

Then came the day . . . when the owner of a small traveling circus offered to trade him a lion for some fancy lettering on his circus wagons.

"A real live lion?" Mr. Yowder asked him.

"Yessir!" the circus man said. "That one right over there," and he pointed out a small beat-up cage on wheels over on the back of the lot.

Now if that had been a cow, a horse, a shoat or some other familiar form of livestock he'd been offered, Mr. Yowder would have examined it very carefully before agreeing to the trade. For it is a well-known fact that such creatures vary widely in value, depending on their age, general health and the condition of their joints, teeth and other parts.

But lions, to the average person, are something special —like Santa Claus, the Government, or the President; mention "lion" to anybody you know (if he's not already in the lion business) and the chances are his eyes will glaze over as he thinks of brass bands, clowns, ladies in pink tights standing tippy-toe on galloping white horses and things like that.

And Mr. Yowder, in that respect, was no different
from anybody else—shrewd trader though he was. He
was so taken with the idea of being the only sign painter
in Missouri—and maybe in the whole United States—to
own a real live lion that it never occurred to him to
suspect that the creature might not really be the bargain
he seemed to be.

So . . . before the man could change his mind Mr.
Yowder shook hands on the deal and hurried off to collect
his lion. When he'd finally gotten the cage hooked behind
his car, he waved good-bye to the circus man and drove

off the lot—without doubt the happiest sign painter in the whole state of Missouri.

As Mr. Yowder knew it would, the story of the sign painter who hauled a lion around in a cage hooked behind his car did spread around the state. But somehow or other the results weren't quite what he'd expected.

The truth was, the lion was unbelievably old and scarred-up. His eyes were bleary and filmed over and most of his yellowed teeth were worn down or broken off, and some skin ailment had laid bare great patches of his hide. His joints were swollen by arthritis or rheumatism or some such trouble so that he walked and moved with great difficulty; and in addition to these things,

probably due to his great age, ailments and slovenly habits, he smelled terrible.

All in all, he was anything but an attractive beast. And Mr. Yowder soon learned that instead of crowding around the cage, as he'd expected, people tended to hold their noses and hurry past—on the upwind side if possible. And children who got too close to the cage were dragged away by their mothers before they caught something dreadful from that "awful animal!"

People wanting signs painted soon began to ask Mr. Yowder to please not bring the old lion with him, or if he did to park the cage around the corner somewhere out of sight. And worse yet, the word began to spread among the loafers in the barber shops and around the filling stations that Mr. Yowder had at last met his match—that he'd been outtraded by a circus man.

By now he was beginning to worry. Not only was the lion making him the laughingstock of the country, he was also eating him out of house and home. Like most folk who have never had any dealings with lions, it had never occurred to him to wonder how much it took to feed one. If he had thought about it at all, he'd probably have supposed that, like his hounds, the animal would be satisfied with table scraps and maybe a beef bone now and again.

But he quickly discovered that his table scraps, even with extra hush puppies thrown in, were only appetizers for that old lion. Some days he ate a half dozen chickens, a turkey or two and maybe a rabbit—and still licked his feed pan hungrily. At the rate Mr. Yowder's supply of livestock was disappearing, he would soon have to begin to think about buying lion feed, which would be expensive as well as difficult to find.

So he began to rack his brain trying to figure some way to get rid of the lion, and if possible to make at least a small profit at the same time. Surely the creature, old as he was, should be good for something.

He advertised LION FOR SALE, CHEAP in both the *Kansas City Star* and *The Grit*, but there didn't seem to be much demand for secondhand lions that year. And it was obvious that the hide wasn't worth lifting, since there wasn't hair enough on it to make a rug.

The only healthy thing about that animal was his roar. When he wasn't eating or sleeping—and being right old he didn't sleep much—he roared. On those swollen arthritic feet he'd shuffle up to one end of the cage and stand looking out over the neighborhood. Then he'd

start pulling himself together. He'd strain until he'd slowly raised his tail to the level of his back, brace himself, take a deep breath, lay back his ears and ROAR. After that he'd drop his tail, stand a moment seeming to be listening to what he'd done, then slowly, and with considerable difficulty, he'd turn around in that narrow cage and get ready to roar again in the other direction.

Day in and day out, night and day, that lion roared on the average of three times an hour, and over a few weeks that adds up to a lot of lion roars.

Up to now, selling lion roars was the only thing Mr. Yowder hadn't considered. But here he was with a lion that was really nothing but a live lion roar factory, so the best thing to do was to try to figure out a way to sell lion roars.

But when he thought about it he realized that there were surprisingly few people in ordinary life who had any real interest in either lions or lion roars. Circuses, however, were another matter—there were dozens of them scattered over the country, and nearly all of them owned from six to forty lions.

As nearly as he could figure the biggest reason for having lions in the circus was so that their roaring in the

menagerie tent just before show time would draw the
crowds to the ticket wagons. Of course ticket selling is a
very important part of the circus business, but Mr.
Yowder knew from experience how much it cost to feed
just one lion. So when he thought about what it was
costing those circuses to feed theirs, he figured they were
paying a terribly high price for their lion roars, even if
they were buying their meat wholesale. It stood to reason
that if somebody came along and showed them how they
could get their lion roars cheaper they'd be glad to talk
business.

So now all Mr. Yowder had to do was figure out a way
to preserve lion roars for later use. If he could do that the
circuses could replace their expensive live lions with
stuffed ones (a first class stuffed lion in those days cost
only ten or twelve dollars) and save a great deal of money.

Then whenever they wanted to draw a crowd all they'd have to do would be to open a can or two of lion roars, and let them out among the cages with the stuffed lions in them.

For several days he spent all his time studying and measuring lion roars as the old lion roared them. He found that a lion roar was usually about four feet seven or eight inches long, and about as big around as his arm. Also, he found, it about ninety-nine percent air.

Now Mr. Yowder knew that it was possible to compress a great deal of air into a very small space, so it was logical to suppose that the same thing could be done with lion roars. But the problem was to find something to put them in once they were compressed.

He thought about that for several days. Then one day he was in the back of Doc Overton's drugstore watching him put up some malaria medicine, scooping the bitter quinine into one half of a gelatine capsule, then slipping the other half on to cap it. And that was when Mr. Yowder got his idea. If he could put each compressed lion roar into its own capsule, all the circus people would have to do when they wanted lion roars would be to throw a handful into a bucket of water. In a few minutes the capsules would dissolve and out would come the lion roars as good as new.

So he bought a box of empty capsules, the biggest Doc had, on credit, and hurried home to try the idea out. On the way he stopped and borrowed an old air compressor that stood behind the filling station and set it up in front

of the lion's cage. After putting an old gramophone horn on the front for the lion to roar into, he started the machine up.

The compressor was a small one, and when the first lion roar started through it the machine banged and rocked, then choked down altogether. Mr. Yowder hadn't realized a lion roar was so tough. So he went back downtown to hunt up a bigger compressor, and it was nearly sundown by the time he got back and the new machine set up. But this time things worked better, and the lion roars went through the compressor without trouble.

But a lion roar, even when compressed, is a little hard to see and at first Mr. Yowder had trouble telling what was lion roar and what was just plain compressed air. However, with practice his judgment improved and he finally caught one and stuffed it into a capsule before it got away.

That was the world's very first Lion Roar Capsule!

All the rest of the afternoon Mr. Yowder compressed lion roars as fast as the old lion roared them. At first he had trouble stuffing a compressed roar into its capsule without breaking part of it off, but by the end of the afternoon he had a half dozen Lion Roar Capsules that looked to be almost perfect.

However, he knew that even the best thought-out
ideas can go wrong, so he decided to try a few of these
capsules out, just to be sure they worked.

Stuffing the little box of Lion Roars in his pocket, he
started to walk to town. On the way he passed the yard
of a lady who had a number of cats she thought right
highly of. They were gathered around a big dish of warm
milk she'd just put out, so Mr. Yowder leaned over the
fence and dropped a Lion Roar Capsule into the dish. For
a minute or two nothing happened and the cats went on
lapping up the milk.

Then the capsule, softened by the milk, suddenly came apart and let the lion roar loose right in the faces of those startled cats! In spite of having been run through an air compressor and then jammed into that small capsule, it was still as fine a lion roar as any one would care to hear.

Mr. Yowder was vastly pleased by this proof that his idea would work, but what the cats thought was another matter. They simply took off in whatever direction they happened to be facing and left that place. A big Persian, finding his way blocked by the sycamore, turned neither to the right nor to the left but climbed straight up to the very topmost twig.

Mr. Yowder also left the neighborhood without delay, and downtown he turned into the alley behind the feed store. The back room was a sort of club for the town checkers players, and while he didn't play checkers himself, he thought it might be a good place to give his Lion Roar Capsules one more tryout.

As he'd expected there were already four men gathered around the old table in a clear space between the stacks of feed and fertilizer. Judge Hapgood and Filthy Bill, the town barber, were playing while a farmer named Rabbit Box Johnson and a drummer from the hotel held down the spectators' chairs. Mr. Yowder said howdy all around and sat down on a bag of oats to watch the game.

Judge Hapgood raised hunting dogs in his spare time and this night he had a fine setter pup lying beside his chair. Later, while the Judge was concentrating on the problem of how to avoid Filthy Bill's move to corner his

king, Mr. Yowder reached out and took the pup in his lap. He petted him a while, then slipped a Lion Roar Capsule well back in his mouth, rubbed his throat until he'd swallowed it and put him back on the floor beside the Judge's chair.

A few moments later, while all four men at the table were concentrating on the Judge's problem, the pup hiccuped as pups are in the habit of doing. But instead of

being an ordinary hiccup this one was a full-sized lion roar. Coming as it did from under the table and echoing back and forth from the walls of that small room, it was truly a fearsome sound—especially to men not familiar with lion roars.

Like the cats earlier in the evening, the checkers players left that place and were across the high loading platform and some yards up the alley before they even tried to disentangle themselves from the table legs and the chairs.

The pup followed them by shortcuts he knew through backyards, and was home scratching on the door by the time the Judge got there. He wasn't hurt, but somehow or other he never did amount to much as a hunting dog— he couldn't stand loud noises of any kind.

Mr. Yowder walked home slowly, dreaming of being rich. He knew now that all he had to do when the circus came to Kansas City in a couple of weeks was go to see the circus men and let them watch while he dropped a handful of Real Roaring Lion Roar Capsules into a bucket of water. When they heard those real lion roars boiling up out of the water as the capsules dissolved, and heard his plan of replacing the expensive live lions with cheap stuffed ones, he'd be in business. Mr. Yowder knew that when fellows like that saw a way to save money they didn't hesitate to take advantage of it. That's how they got rich enough to go into the circus business in the first place.

After that Mr. Yowder stopped painting signs entirely
and spent all his time compressing lion roars. So by the
time Circus Day came he had about seventy dozen Lion
Roar Capsules put away in the cellar where it was cool.
He didn't know if they'd spoil, but he was taking no
chances.

He'd had a printer print up some handsome gummed
labels that said YOWDER'S REAL ROARING LION ROAR
CAPSULES in red letters. And Doc Overton had sold him
some little cardboard boxes with partitions inside to keep
the capsules from rattling around. Each box held thirty-
six compressed lion roars, and Mr. Yowder figured the
circus people would be glad to pay at least fifty cents a
roar.

Right after breakfast on Circus Day he fed the old lion, carried the boxes of lion roars out of the cellar and loaded them into the back of his old car. What with one thing and another all these chores had taken a good deal of time, and so it was after noon before he finally got onto the road.

As he drove along he thought about the stories that would be told around over the country about how he had made a fortune out of the beat-up old lion nobody else wanted. Now and again he heard a little thunder behind him, but the sun was shining where he was so he didn't pay it much mind.

It was just before he came to the bridge across the Little Blue River, about where the Raytown Road turns off, that somebody's old hound trotted out onto the road ahead and stopped, looking the other way.

To avoid hitting the hound Mr. Yowder stepped hard on the brakes, and by the time he'd stopped he found himself soaked to the skin by heavy rain. Looking around he found the back of the car full of water to the tops of the doors and the lion roar boxes afloat.

What had happened was that for some time he'd been driving just in the front edge of one of the small but violent rainstorms that are common in that country. Until he'd slowed for the hound, rain had been falling steadily into the backseat, but none into the front. Such things can happen in Missouri.

Mr. Yowder tried to save some of the floating boxes but the cardboard was already soaked, and the capsules themselves were beginning to soften. While he watched, the first lion roar came bubbling up from among the sodden boxes and roared off across Jackson County. It was closely followed by another, and in what seemed to Mr. Yowder to be only seconds his lion roars were streaking away in all directions. There was nothing he could do but hold his hands over his ears and let them go.

It is a well-established fact that a lion roar can be heard for about a mile and a half on a quiet day, so it is reasonable to suppose that several end to end could be heard much farther. And here were lion roars going out in strings of a dozen or more in any direction you wanted to listen, so there is no telling just how far away that uproar was heard.

Horses ran away with farmers in the fields, windows
shattered, dogs and chickens went under the houses and
refused to come out for days after. Even old Granny
North, who hadn't heard a word anyone said to her for
over forty years, claimed she'd heard lion roars roaring
by her house in Lone Jack that day. It was told later that

down Knob Noster Way the sky turned black as night and
a great wind came up. It could have been so, but stories do
tend to grow in the telling after any such catastrophe.
However, it was generally agreed that there hadn't been
such excitement in that part of the country since Quan-
trill's last raid, back in Jayhawker days.

When the last of his lion roars had finally gone out of hearing, Mr. Yowder sat for a while waiting for the ringing to leave his ears. Then he got out, cranked up his car and turned back for home.

This was a terrible setback to his plans for going into the lion roar business, but he figured he still had his lion and he should be able to replace the lost lion roars in time to meet the circus again when it showed in Jefferson City later in the summer.

However, it turned out that his troubles were still not over.

When he drove into the yard, the first thing he noticed was that the lion's cage was empty. Looking closer he found that the rotten floorboards had finally given way beneath the old lion's weight, and he'd fallen out through the bottom. Nowhere was he to be seen. Mr. Yowder was still searching the sheds and hen houses when he heard the train whistle.

Looking across the little pasture he saw the old lion standing on the railroad embankment beyond. Somehow, old and crippled with rheumatism as he was, and half-blind besides, that feeble old creature had managed to get through the wire fence and up the steep embankment, and now stood braced squarely between the rails, facing the oncoming train!

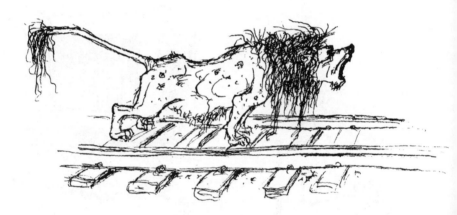

It was a fast freight with two locomotives, and while the whistles screamed and sparks flew from the brake shoes and sliding wheels, the old lion began to pull himself together. He slowly raised his head, stiffened his tail straight out behind him, opened his mouth wide and finally ROARED right in the oncoming locomotive's face!

The train didn't stop and for a while there was nothing to be seen through the clouds of steam, dust and coal smoke. Then, after the last of the hundred and seventy-two cars and the caboose had passed, Mr. Yowder slowly climbed the bank and looked about.

But there was nothing left of the lion except for a few scattered bits and pieces, and a few tufts of coarse tawny hair caught on nearby bushes.

Mr. Yowder carefully gathered up all the bits he could find and buried them in a small grave beside the right of way.

Later he traded a sign for a small white monument with TO THE MEMORY OF A BRAVE LION carved onto it and set it up to mark the spot. It can still be seen, if you look close, a few feet to the right of milepost 623 beside the tracks of the Kansas, Topeka and Santa Fe.

Losing the lion put Mr. Yowder out of the lion roar
business, of course. As far as anyone knows he gave up all
hopes of ever being rich, and probably is still painting
signs somewhere in Missouri, or Kansas, or Oklahoma or
some such place.

MR. YOWDER
AND THE
STEAMBOAT

Mr. Xenon Zebulon Yowder always spoke of himself as being THE WORLD'S BESTEST AND FASTEST SIGN PAINTER, and perhaps he was.

His usual home range was west of Kansas City, Missouri, south to Texas, north to Montana and the Dakotas, and west as far as his fancy might take him.

But at the time I speak of, he was wintering in New York City, New York. That is about as far east as one can get, but how it came about he never did say. It seems,

however, that he'd rented him a nice room in a boarding house not far from one of the two rivers that run on either side of that town.

The way Mr. Yowder told it later, his adventure with the steamboat started one morning when he happened to ask his landlady, a widow woman named O'Leary, if there were any fish down there in the river. She said the fishing was known to be very good at that time of year, and should Mr. Yowder take a notion to go catch a mess, she'd cook them up for his supper.

Mr. Yowder had always liked to fish, so he borrowed a fish pole the landlady had stored in the basement and hurried down to the river right after breakfast.

But he found all the good places along the bank were
already taken, so he decided to rent him a rowboat, figur-
ing that there should be plenty of good fishing holes fur-
ther out in the river.

There are not many places in a town like New York
City, New York, where a man can dig fishing worms, so
to save time, he bought some from the man that rented
him the boat.

The man explained how the oars worked, and after Mr. Yowder had gotten himself settled on the seat, he pushed the boat loose from the bank and waved good-bye.

At first Mr. Yowder had some trouble trying to pull on the oars while looking back over his shoulder to see where he was going. But soon he got the hang of it and rowed briskly out into the river.

However, finding a quiet fishing hole turned out to be no easy matter, for that river was crowded with boats. There were boats of all sizes, he said—small, middle-sized

and so big you'd not believe it. And they were going in all directions. There were boats going upstream, and there were boats going downstream. There were boats going back and forth across the river, and still others that didn't seem to be going anywhere in particular—just messing around.

Mr. Yowder would no sooner find himself what looked like a good place to fish and start baiting his hook, than he'd hear the roar of a whistle and look up to find himself directly in the path of a boat bigger than Bearpaw Smith's store back home in Lonetree County. He spent most of his time rowing frantically, first in one direction and then the other, to keep from being run over.

For a while he was so busy trying to keep out of the way of all those boats, that he didn't notice the brisk current carrying him towards the mouth of the river. But when he did have time to stop and look around, he found he was a mile or two below town and well out onto the ocean—which he'd never seen before. At last he'd gotten away from the boats; there wasn't one in sight anywhere.

But even so, his troubles were not over—he quickly discovered that the ocean is by no means flat like one expects water to be. Instead, it was all hills—hills of water in any direction he looked. And worst of all, the hills did not stay still. He'd no sooner row up to the top of one and stop to look around, than the thing would slither out from under his boat and leave him in a swale again!

He rowed this way and that way, up one hill and down another, looking for a level place where he could stop and fish. But there were no level places—nothing but

water going uphill and downhill. And then, for some reason, his stomach began to feel a little queasy, so he decided he'd best turn around and go back.

But when he looked around, he discovered he was out of sight of land. Of course there were no signposts out there, nor any landmarks of any kind, so he had no idea how he was going to find the way back to town.

He was lost.

But about that time, he saw a big steamboat standing still in the water off to his left a half a mile away. So he decided to row over and ask them the way to town.

When Mr. Yowder got up close to the steamboat, he couldn't see anybody on it. But he hollered and banged on the side with an oar, and pretty soon a man wearing a cap with a lot of gold embroidery on it leaned over the rail and asked him what he wanted.

Mr. Yowder explained that he was lost, and could the man direct him to New York City, New York.

The fellow explained that he was Captain of the steamboat and was going that way himself, just as soon as his hired man fixed the engine trouble they were having at the moment. He went on to say that if Mr. Yowder wasn't in a big hurry, he was welcome to tie his boat on behind and ride back to town with him. So Mr. Yowder tied his boat to a long rope hanging down at the back of the steamboat, and the Captain let down a ladder so he could climb up on top.

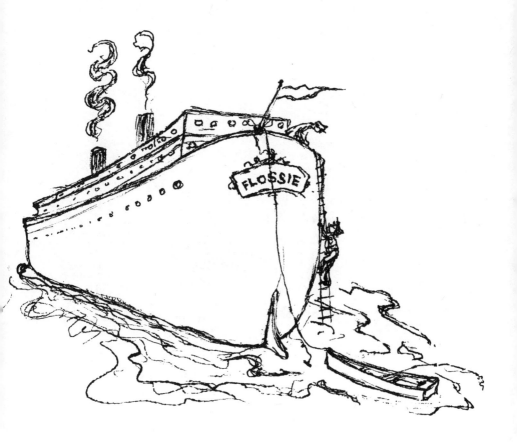

Mr. Yowder remarked that he was right handy with machinery himself, so he and the Captain went downstairs to where they kept the engine, to see if they could help the hired man.

The three of them, working together, soon found the trouble and got the thing to running. It still missed on one cylinder, but the Captain said it should get them into New York City all right. So leaving the hired man to run the engine, the Captain and Mr. Yowder went back upstairs to what the Captain called the Bridge. That was the place he drove the steamboat from.

It was a room with big windows, high up in the front of the boat. The Captain walked up to a steering wheel as high as he was, looked at a big compass to see which way the steamboat was pointing, then hollered down a speaking tube and told the hired man he was ready to start.

He turned the steering wheel this way and that for a while, until he had the steamboat going the way he wanted, but after that there wasn't much to do. So he brushed some maps and newspapers off a little table, got out some cards and asked Mr. Yowder if he'd like to play a few games just to pass the time. Mr. Yowder explained that he wasn't much of a card player, but if they just played for matches, it was all right with him.

That steamboat was so big, it sort of cut through the
hills of water instead of going up and down like Mr.
Yowder's rowboat had done, and his stomach began to
feel better.

Sometimes, when it was Mr. Yowder's deal, the Captain
would get up to speak down the speaking tube to the
hired man about the engine, or to blow the whistle at
some boat going by. But mostly they just played cards.

At first they played for matches, but after a while the
Captain suggested playing for money—nickels and dimes,
perhaps—just to make the game more interesting.

It turned out that the Captain wasn't a very good card
player, and before long Mr. Yowder had won all the
change he had on him—a dollar and seventy-six cents, his

penknife and a gold-trimmed goose quill toothpick he was very proud of.

Then they played for the Captain's official gold-embroidered captain's cap, and Mr. Yowder won again.

When Mr. Yowder took off his old Stetson and saw himself in the mirror wearing that fancy cap, he was right pleased with the change in his appearance.

The Captain still did not want to stop playing, so next they played for his license to drive steamboats, and Mr. Yowder won again. He had never seen a steamboat driver's license before and was busy reading all the fancy words on it, when the Captain looked out the window and said, "There comes the Pilot."

"What's a Pilot?" Mr. Yowder wanted to know, and the Captain explained to him that a Captain could drive a steamboat back and forth across the ocean, but couldn't drive it up to the bank and tie it up. The Pilot had to do that.

The Pilot had just climbed up the ladder, when the hired man hollered up the speaking tube that the engine

was broken down again. He figured it would take a half hour or so to fix it, so the Captain got another chair and invited the Pilot to take a hand in their card game while they waited.

On the first hand, the Pilot bet a nickel, and Mr. Yowder bet the same. The Captain said all he had left was the steamboat, and was it all right if he bet that.

The Pilot told the Captain he couldn't bet the steamboat because he didn't own it—he just drove it for the man that did. So the Pilot and Mr. Yowder played cards, while the Captain looked out the window and drummed his fingers on the sill.

It turned out that the Pilot was no better a card player than the Captain had been. By the time the hired man called up through the speaking tube to say he had the engine running again, Mr. Yowder had won all his small change, his fancy sailor-type jackknife, his official pilot's cap and his license to drive steamboats up to the bank.

So Mr. Yowder put on his new pilot's cap, stuffed the licenses into his hip pocket and said, "Well, I reckon I'd best start this thing towards town if we're going to get there by suppertime." And he walked over to the big steering wheel and picked up the speaking tube to tell the hired man to start things up.

The Captain and the Pilot raised considerable objection to his taking over the driving, but Mr. Yowder pointed out to them the rule that said it was against the law for anybody to drive a steamboat without a license—and he was the only man there that had one. It didn't seem right to them, somehow, but they had to admit that he did have the licenses, and the official caps that went with them.

Mr. Yowder had a little trouble at first, trying to steer in a straight line, never having driven a steamboat before. But by the time he'd come in sight of town, he wasn't

doing too badly. He blew the whistle a lot, and that helped him miss the boats that got in his way.

The place where he was supposed to tie the steamboat to the bank was a couple of miles up the river, at the far end of town. But Mr. Yowder could see that the river was still swarming with boats of all sizes up that way, and decided to take a shortcut.

Just before he passed the Statue of Liberty they have there, he hauled the big steering wheel clear over to the right and headed straight for the little park where Broadway Street comes down to the end of the island the town is built on.

The Captain and the Pilot began to fuss and carry on something dreadful, claiming that Mr. Yowder was going to wreck the steamboat.

Mr. Yowder told them he was doing no such thing— he was just taking a shortcut up Broadway Street. Not only would it be quicker, but he could let the passengers off right at their hotels on the way and save them taxi fares.

He also reminded them that the rule book said arguing with a steamboat Captain was called MUTINY, a very serious crime.

It took Mr. Yowder two tries to get the steamboat up
onto the bank, but he finally made it and steered right up
the middle of Broadway Street. It was a splendid sight to
see, he told us later. Black smoke poured out of the
steamboat's chimneys, and clouds of sparks flew from
underneath where the iron bottom screeched along the
cobblestones. But from the way the people in the little
park and the crowds along the street carried on, you'd
have thought nobody had ever driven a steamboat up
Broadway before!

Policemen held up their hands and blew their whistles,
dogs barked and snapped at the strange monster while
automobiles, taxis and trucks tangled fenders as they

ducked into alleys and side streets or drove up onto the sidewalks to get out of the steamboat's way.

At the bend where Wall Street and Broadway come together, the high buildings are right close together, but Mr. Yowder managed to steer the steamboat between them without doing any damage except for knocking down some flagpoles that stuck out over the street, and startling a windowwasher working on a high ledge.

Once around the bend, the street was much wider, and he made better time.

But then the steamboat began to run into some of the thousands of wires that are strung like clotheslines across

the street in New York City. They are fastened to cross
arms at the tops of high poles out of the way of ordinary
traffic, but still too low for a steamboat to go under. Mr.
Yowder hated to tear them down, but there was nothing
else he could do, so he kept on driving.

Before long there were telephone wires, electric wires
and cables of all sizes hanging from the front of the steamboat and streaming behind for blocks. The fellows that
owned them were running alongside waving their arms,
shouting things Mr. Yowder couldn't hear. But he figured
it was their fault for hanging their wires too low in the
first place, so he pulled the whistle cord a time or two, in
a friendly way, and drove on.

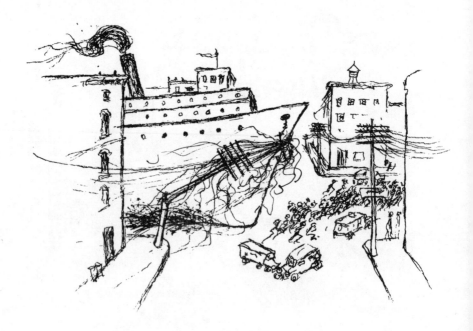

He was just about to ask the Captain which hotel he should stop at first, when he steered around an easy bend and saw an iron bridge across the street ahead. It was the first he knew of the elevated railroad that ran all over New York City, on tracks built high above the streets.

The Captain and the Pilot knew that the steamboat didn't have any brakes, so they cracked their knuckles and squinched their eyes shut while they waited for the crash. After a quick look, Mr. Yowder decided he just might be able to squeeze the steamboat under the bridge. He knew it would probably knock the boat's chimneys down, but stovepipe isn't expensive. So he called down

the speaking tube for the hired man to give him full speed, blew the whistle real loud and drove straight ahead.

But he had misjudged the height of the steamboat by four and a half inches, they found out later. So when the screeching and squealing of bending iron was over and the dust had begun to settle, the steamboat was jammed under the bridge, tight as a cork in a bottle, completely blocking the street.

Mr. Yowder tried every way he knew to get that steamboat loose. He called down to the hired man to put the engine in reverse, while people in the street put their shoulders against the front end of the boat and pushed. But nothing worked. Even blowing the whistle didn't help.

Then he asked the Captain to hand him the Owner's Manual and Instruction Book that had come with the steamboat when it was new. It told how to get loose from mudbanks, what to do when two boats ran into each other at sea, and things like that. But nowhere was there a word about how to get out from under a railroad bridge.

Neither the Captain nor the Pilot had ever seen such an accident before, so they couldn't help him.

Mr. Yowder finally decided that the only thing to do was to call the hired man upstairs and have him go to the livery stable for a team of horses to pull the steamboat loose.

The hired man said he didn't know where the livery stable was, but Mr. Yowder told him just to ask a policeman. There were dozens of them down on the street waving their hands, blowing their whistles and looking in rule books.

So the Captain hung the ladder over the side of the steamboat, and the hired man climbed down, asked directions from a policeman, and started off downtown to get the team of horses.

After the hired man was gone, Mr. Yowder gave the
Captain and the Pilot back their official caps and their
licenses, and put his battered Stetson back on. He thanked
them for the ride and told them if they were ever out west
of Kansas City, Missouri, to be sure to look him up.

"You're not going away leaving this boat stuck here,
are you?" they wanted to know.

"It'll take an hour or two to get the horses here to pull
it loose," Mr. Yowder told them. "And I'm renting this
rowboat by the hour, so I have to hurry to get it back to
the man I rented it from, before he closes up for the
night."

The Captain and the Pilot both begged him to stay and help them, but he said he'd already done all he could for them. He climbed down the ladder, and the last they saw of him, he was walking toward the river dragging his rented rowboat behind him.

As far as anybody knows, neither the Pilot nor the Captain every played cards again.

MR. YOWDER
AND THE
GIANT BULL SNAKE

At the time I speak of (which was a long time ago), that part of the country known as THE GREAT PLAINS was still mostly uninhabited.

It seemed an unlikely place to find a sign painter, but nonetheless Mr. Xenon Zebulon Yowder, who even then spoke of himself as "The World's Bestest and Fastest Sign Painter," was there. He wasn't going anywhere in particular, just taking himself a trip to see the country.

An occasional adventurous settler plowed up small patches of sod fenced in with barbed wire, Indians chased buffalo—or the settlers' livestock—and were themselves chased by soldiers.

But in that vast treeless land such scattered activities went almost unnoticed, and the general impression was of a place where nobody lived and where nothing ever happened.

When he ran short of flour, coffee, or other supplies, Mr. Yowder might join one of the wagon trains crossing the plains on the way to Oregon or California and paint PIKES PEAK OR BUST, WE ARE FROM OHIO, and other such sayings in fancy letters on the wagons in return for what he needed.

Other times he made a little money painting road signs pointing to water holes, short cuts, or good camping places.

But mostly he rode alone, just exploring the country and thinking of the stories he'd have to tell later.

One afternoon, near the headwaters of The Powder River—or maybe it was Pumpkin Creek (he had no map and couldn't be right sure)—Mr. Yowder shot two fat prairie hens and made camp by a small clear spring. After picketing his horse on good grass, he'd built a fire, put the birds on to cook and was leaning back against his saddle, taking a rest, when he first noticed the little snake.

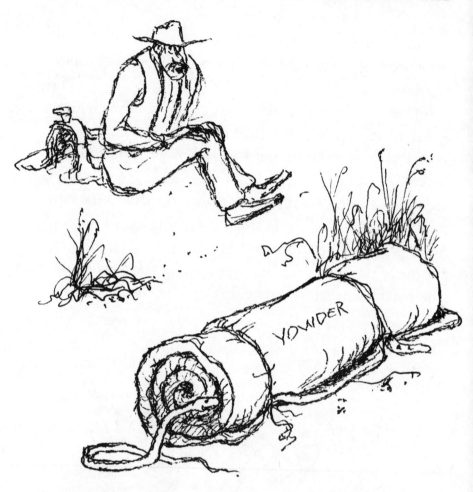

As was usual for that time of year—it was late spring by
the way—hundreds of newly hatched bull snakes were
going about their business in the tall grass, learning the
bull snake trade. And now one of these had come up to
the other side of the fire and was investigating Mr.
Yowder's bedding roll.

Mr. Yowder liked all sorts of animals, even snakes, so he watched as this one tested and tasted each string and strap with his flickering forked tongue.

But when the snake started to crawl inside the blanket roll, he spoke up. "You'd better stay out of that, Snake," he said in snake. "That there's my bed."

The little snake was somewhat startled by hearing a man speaking his language, and scuttled into the grass. But he quickly returned, stuck his head up and asked, "Where did you learn to talk snake?"

"I worked one time down in Oklahoma territory, painting signs along the 'Strip,' " Mr. Yowder told him. "Were a sight of snakes there, and almost no people, so if I wanted anybody to talk to, I had to learn snake."

That seemed reasonable to the little bull snake, and he curled up by the fire to listen to Mr. Yowder's tales of the places he'd been and the stange things he'd seen.

When the birds were cooked Mr. Yowder ate his supper, now and then cutting off small slivers of meat for

the snake, who now was busily telling how dull bull snake life was thereabouts. He explained that he was ambitious —which was unusual for a snake—and he hoped to see the world and maybe become famous when he was bigger.

Mr. Yowder was impressed, but he couldn't see much chance for a snake to become famous out in that country.

All in all, however, they both enjoyed the talk, and just before dark the little bull snake went off home to bed, his head full of the stories Mr. Yowder had told him.

Out on the plain nearby was a high rock—a landmark
that could be seen for miles—and Mr. Yowder spent nearly
a week painting YOWDER THE SIGN PAINTER WAS HERE
in large fancy letters up near the top of it. That sign,
though faded by wind and rain, could still be read by
passersby until about eight years ago.

And every afternoon when Mr. Yowder came back to camp, the little snake was there to meet him. One day Mr. Yowder said to him, "It don't seem right to just keep calling you 'Snake.' You need a name. So if you don't mind, I'm going to call you Knute, after my old uncle back in Missouri."

Of course the snake was right pleased, for none of his friends or relations had names, or even nicknames.

Sitting by the small fire, the man and the snake would talk for hours, or Mr. Yowder would read aloud from some tattered magazines he had in his pack. The snake liked Western stories, but best of all he liked the magazine that told of people who started out puny but later took body-building courses and became so strong no bully ever again dared kick sand in their faces. Over and over, he had Mr. Yowder read him the story of how Mr. Teddy Roosevelt took exercises and became President of the United States.

When Knute suggested that maybe Mr. Yowder could send off and get him one of those body-building courses, Mr. Yowder explained to him that, there being no post office on the Great Plains as yet, it would be difficult to either send or receive mail. Besides, those courses were probably pretty expensive.

But when he saw how disappointed Knute was, he suggested that, exercise being the main part of body-building, maybe between them they could invent some of their own.

For a start he pointed to two tall weeds standing about
the snake's length apart, and showed Knute how to
hook his neck around one, and take a hitch with his tail
around the other. Then he told him to flex all his muscles
and try to pull the tops together, relax, then pull again.

In a few minutes the snake was out of breath, not being used to any exercise more violent than wriggling through the grass, hunting for birds' eggs, grasshoppers, and other small game. He dropped to the ground, and for a while lay panting.

The next day the little snake's muscles were stiff and
sore, and Mr. Yowder expected him to give up the body-
building idea then and there. But Knute was indeed an
unusual snake, and hour after hour—while his friends and
relatives took naps, or lay about in the sun—he did his
exercises.

All that exercise, however, gave him a tremendous
appetite. So when he wasn't exercising he was hunting for
something to eat, and he began to grow faster than any
snake on the Great Plains. Every afternoon, near sundown, he would make a full-length impression of his
body on a patch of white sand near his den to mark the
progress of his body-building.

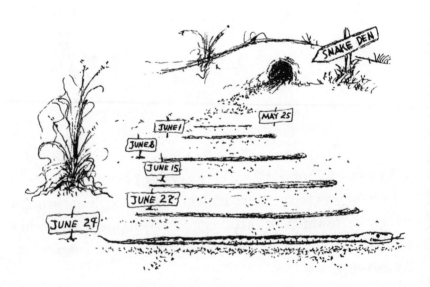

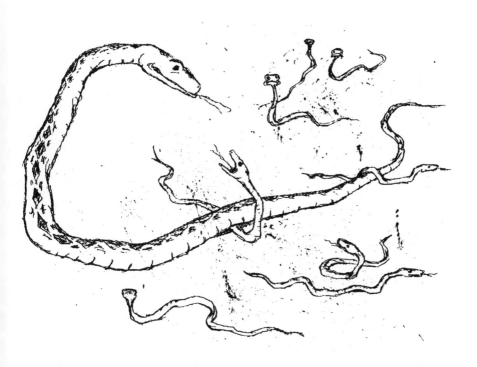

By the time Mr. Yowder began to think of drifting south to find work for the winter, Knute was already many times larger than any snake in the neighborhood. And he told Mr. Yowder that the others had begun to complain that he was all the time running over them, knocking them down, spraining their backs, or kicking dust in their eyes.

So, much as he disliked the idea of leaving home, it looked as if he'd have to find a place where there was more room for a snake his size.

Knute was very good company, and Mr. Yowder enjoyed having someone to talk to. Besides that, he caught his own food. So Mr. Yowder suggested that they travel south together. The snake was pleased by the chance to see the world. While Mr. Yowder saddled his horse and rolled up his camp outfit, Knute went to tell his friends and relations good-bye. He said he'd try to let them know if he found work, and the last they ever saw of him he was racing along beside Mr. Yowder's horse.

Mr. Yowder was in no hurry, so Knute had plenty of time to hunt for food and to keep up his body-building exercises as well. Before they rode into any of the small towns along the way, Mr. Yowder would take the snake up and hang him from the saddle horn like a coil of old rope. That saved them much trouble from dogs, constables, and people who simply disliked snakes.

At Abilene, Kansas—or maybe it was Dodge City—Mr. Yowder decided they were far enough south. He and the snake moved into an abandoned shack a mile or so out of town and settled down for the winter.

Every morning after breakfast Mr. Yowder let Knute out to hunt in the open country to the west, while he himself spent the day in town, painting signs or playing cards.

By Chrismas, however, Mr. Yowder began to wonder
if maybe he hadn't made a mistake starting Knute on the
body-building idea. For the snake continued to grow,
and by Groundhog Day was so long that, by the time
he had looped and coiled himself around inside the shack,
getting himself comfortable for the night, there was very
little room left for Mr. Yowder. And there was also the
danger that he might accidentally knock over the stove
or upset the lantern and set the place afire.

But luckily spring came early, and Mr. Yowder and the snake went back to camping on the prairie as they'd done before. Mr. Yowder got a job with the railroad, painting numbers on mileposts and names on the little stations along the tracks.

While Mr. Yowder worked, Knute hunted and exercised as usual. But in the afternoons he liked to lie with his body out of sight behind a low hill, his chin resting flat on the crest, and watch the long trains go puffing by.

Things went well enough with Mr. Yowder and the snake during the early spring, until the night a violent thunder and lightning storm stampeded a trail herd of Texas longhorns being held nearby. The cattle missed Mr. Yowder's camp, but in the excitement his horse got loose and was never seen again.

Mr. Yowder disliked the idea of walking to his work, so one day he asked Knute if he'd mind trying the saddle on for size. The snake didn't mind, and Mr. Yowder strapped it on the snake's neck, just behind his head. When the man had his feet in the stirrups, the snake raised his head and they went for a short ride. The saddle fit just fine.

Every morning after that, Mr. Yowder rode to wherever he was working, then turned Knute loose to hunt, after telling him where to meet him at quitting time.

At first the train crews were a little startled by the sight of Mr. Yowder riding along beside the tracks on the giant snake, but they soon got used to the idea and always waved when they went by.

However, Easterners, politicians, and other such folk never did quite believe their eyes.

Knute was living almost entirely on buffalo by then, and when he had time Mr. Yowder often rode along while the snake did his day's hunting. After Knute had fed, if Mr. Yowder needed meat for himself or to give to his friends among the train crews, he would shoot a fat buffalo and carry the meat home strapped behind his saddle.

The snake had a smooth gait and, shooting from his high perch, Mr. Yowder seldom missed.

One day, on the way back from one of their hunts, Mr. Yowder and Knute came over a low hill and met a patrol

of the soldiers who usually spent all of their time chasing
Indians around the country. The soldiers had never seen
so large a snake, nor even heard tell of one, so they and
their horses were considerably upset.

But after Mr. Yowder dismounted and had Knute
back down the slope out of sight, both men and horses
quieted down. The General in command had heard
stories about the man and the snake who hunted buffalo,
and now he walked up to shake hands with Mr. Yowder
and get a closer look at Knute.

The General was a man who was seldom surprised by
anything, but even so he could hardly believe his ears
when he heard Mr. Yowder and Knute talking snake.

After his first surprise, the General got right down to business, as is the way with generals. It seemed that Mr. Buffalo Bill, who was the Army's official buffalo hunter, had joined a wild West show and gone back east and other places. So the fort was running out of meat, and the General had had to put most of his soldiers to work hunting buffalo.

But it turned out the soldiers were not very good buffalo hunters. They talked loud, and the rattling of their spurs, sabers, and other gear often frightened herds a half a mile away. And when they did get close, they found that their cavalry horses panicked at the sight and smell of buffalo. So, what with one thing and another, the cooks at the fort still had almost nothing to cook, and the soldiers were beginning to complain.

Besides that, with the soldiers spending all of their time trying to shoot buffalo, there was nobody left to chase the

Indians. So they were getting fat and lazy, spending their time in their tepees taking naps, telling stories, or gambling. And of course the Government didn't like that. So what the General wanted was to hire Mr. Yowder and the snake to take Mr. Buffalo Bill's place hunting buffalo for the Army so the soldiers could get back to chasing Indians, which was what they were paid for.

Mr. Yowder told the General things were a little slow in the sign painting business right then and, as far as he was concerned, he'd be pleased to help the Army out. But naturally he'd have to talk it over with the snake first.

After Mr. Yowder had explained to him what the General had in mind, Knute thought for a while and decided he sort of liked the idea of being the only snake in the world working for the Government. So he and Mr. Yowder took Mr. Buffalo Bill's place as official buffalo hunters for the United States Army.

It was a grand sight to see them leave for work of a morning. No matter how early the hour or bad the weather the General, in his nightshirt, stood by the fort gates to wave good-bye. Behind the General the band

would be playing "Garry Owen," "The Yellow Rose of Texas," and other loud tunes that soldiers like.

The mule teams pulling the line of wagons that would haul the meat back, and the horses of the butchers and buffalo skinners who rode alongside, stirred up a cloud of dust that almost hid Knute as he moved along the column. The great snake arched his neck like a proud horse, while Mr. Yowder sat straight in his saddle, holding his favorite buffalo gun in one hand and the staff of the flag the General had given them in the other.

As soon as they were out of sight of the fort, Knute and Mr. Yowder would go on ahead while the wagons followed, for the snake traveled much faster than the horses and mules. When they found buffalo, Knute would circle the herd, completely hemming it in, while Mr. Yowder sat in the saddle and shot as many as the Army wagons could haul away.

When that was done, Mr. Yowder would build a little fire and pile a bunch of green sage on it to make a smoke signal to guide the wagons following them. Then he and Knute would stretch out on the grass and rest until the

butchers and skinners had finished their work. Later, when the wagons were loaded down with meat and hides, the man and snake would lead the way back to the fort.

It was a good job and Knute and Mr. Yowder might have been working for the Army yet, but Mr. Buffalo Bill got tired of the wild West show (the long hours and all) and asked for his job back, hunting buffalo for the Army.

The General knew that Knute and Mr. Yowder were really bringing in more meat than Mr. Buffalo Bill had done. But on the other hand, Mr. Buffalo Bill was now a very famous person, and he had just explained to the Gen-

eral that the President of the United States—who was a personal friend of Mr. Buffalo Bill's—along with a train-load of senators, governors, and newspaper writers, was coming out to the fort the very next day to watch Mr. Buffalo Bill shoot buffalo. A general, if he wants to keep on being a general, needs to be friendly to such people, so he told Mr. Yowder and Knute he was sorry but he'd have to pay them off.

Mr. Yowder and the snake went back to their camp behind the fort to talk things over. Nobody had told them that the President of the United States was coming to the fort to watch Mr. Buffalo Bill shoot buffalo the next day. But the General had paid them for the full week, even though it was only Friday—and they felt they owed the Government the extra day's work they had already been paid for.

So early the next morning, without saying anything to anybody, they set off by themselves on their last day's work for the Government.

About midmorning, Mr. Yowder and Knute found the biggest buffalo herd they'd ever seen—they couldn't guess how many, but there must have been thousands, or maybe a million—on the head of Sand Creek, some miles beyond the Box Elder. This time they had no wagons along, or men to skin the buffalo and load the meat, so they decided to slowly drive the whole herd right up to the gate of the fort before Mr. Yowder started shooting.

It was a little before noon when the President of the United States and his party drove out from town. They shook hands with Mr. Buffalo Bill, were introduced to the General, and listened to a short band concert. Then one of Mr. Buffalo Bill's Indian scouts rode up on a sweaty horse, saying a herd of buffalo was just coming into the wide valley of Box Elder Creek only a couple of miles away.

Mr. Buffalo Bill mounted his white horse, waved his favorite buffalo gun over his head, and told the President of the United States and the other important people to get into the wagons and follow him to the top of the nearby ridge, where there would be a good view of the herd. As soon as they were in place, he'd show them how he, The Greatest Buffalo Hunter in the United States of America, and perhaps the greatest in the world, went about his work.

Little did Mr. Buffalo Bill know that the buffalo herd was being driven by Knute and Mr. Yowder. Nor did he know that a piece of paper blowing in the grass had just stampeded the herd.

And directly in the path of those thousands of mad-
dened beasts were Mr. Buffalo Bill, himself, and the
President of the United States, as well as all the other
important people!

When the leaders of the stampeding herd roared over the ridge ahead of him, Mr. Buffalo Bill did his best, but as soon as he shot one a hundred more took its place. The huge dust cloud hid what was happening, and all one could hear was the bellowing of buffalo, the shouting of men (the President's voice loudest of all), the thunder of buffalo hooves, and the breaking of wood as the wagons were overturned and trampled into kindling.

How long the stampede lasted nobody remembers, but when Knute and Mr. Yowder looked over the ridge into the slowly settling cloud of dust, they saw broken, over-

turned wagons, runaway horses, and torn flags and strips of bunting scattered over the slopes below. Mr. Buffalo Bill, his white hat black with dust, was stamping about, waving his hands and kicking at the dead buffalo lying about.

The General and a couple of governors were dusting the President of the United States off, pinning up the rips in his coat, and trying to find his hat. But nobody was badly hurt, and Mr. Yowder saw there was really nothing he could do to help, so he and Knute quietly turned around and went back the way they'd come.

Neither Mr. Yowder nor the giant bull snake were ever seen in those parts again. Some say that Knute finally settled in South America, where large snakes are not uncommon. Others have it that he went east and got into the sea serpent business—but nobody knows for sure.

Mr. Yowder later became famous as The World's Fastest and Bestest Sign Painter, but it is a well known fact that he never after that talked snake. Nor did he ever again have dealings with the United States Army.